GO GREEN! LEAD THE WAY

Catherine Chambers

Crabtree Publishing Company

www.crabtreebooks.com

Author: Catherine Chambers
Editor: Crystal Sikkens
Project coordinator: Kathy Middleton
Production coordinator: Ken Wright
Prepress technician: Margaret Amy Salter
Series consultant: Gill Matthews

Picture credits:
Dreamstime: Mika Specta 17, Mark Yuill 12
Istockphoto: Ian Hamilton 13, David Parsons 14
Shutterstock: (Cover) Melissa Schalke top, Kyle Smith bottom; Mark Atkins 11, Hagit Berkovich 7, Archana Bhartia 15, Sebastien Burel 6, Victor Burnside 21t, Terrance Emerson 10, Eray Haciosmanoglu 16, Cheryl Hill 4, Palis Michael 5, Norman Pogson 21b, Jose AS Reyes 9b, Christina Richards 20, Mark William Richardson 18, Otmar Smit 9t

Library and Archives Canada Cataloguing in Publication

Chambers, Catherine, 1954-
Go green! Lead the way / Catherine Chambers.

(Crabtree connections)
Includes index.
ISBN 978-0-7787-9947-4 (bound).--ISBN 978-0-7787-9969-6 (pbk.)

1. Environmentalism--Juvenile literature.
2. Green movement--Juvenile literature. I. Title.
II. Series: Crabtree connections.

GE195.5.C43 2010 j333.72 C2010-901521-5

Library of Congress Cataloging-in-Publication Data

Chambers, Catherine, 1954-
Go green! lead the way / Catherine Chambers.
p. cm. -- (Crabtree connections)
Includes index.
ISBN 978-0-7787-9969-6 (pbk. : alk. paper) -- ISBN 978-0-7787-9947- (reinforced library binding : alk. paper)
1. Environmentalism--Juvenile literature. 2. Green movement--Juvenile literature. I. Title. II. Series.

GE195.5.C53 2011
333.72--dc22

2010008066

Crabtree Publishing Company

www.crabtreebooks.com 1-800-387-7650

Printed in the USA / 122016 / CG20161021

Published in Canada
Crabtree Publishing
616 Welland Ave.
St. Catharines, Ontario
L2M 5V6

Published in the United States
Crabtree Publishing
PMB 59051
350 Fifth Avenue, 59th Floor
New York, New York 10118

CONTENTS

WHY SHOULD WE CARE?

Our precious planet is changing fast. The weather is more extreme and natural landscapes are disappearing. It is also getting harder to grow enough food to feed everyone.

What's the problem?

Earth has heated up over the last 200 years. This is because we've burned a lot of **fossil fuels,** such as coal and oil. This releases gases that trap heat inside our **atmosphere**.

Think about how you would feel if this mountain lost its snow or the trees died. Do you want to do something to help our planet now?

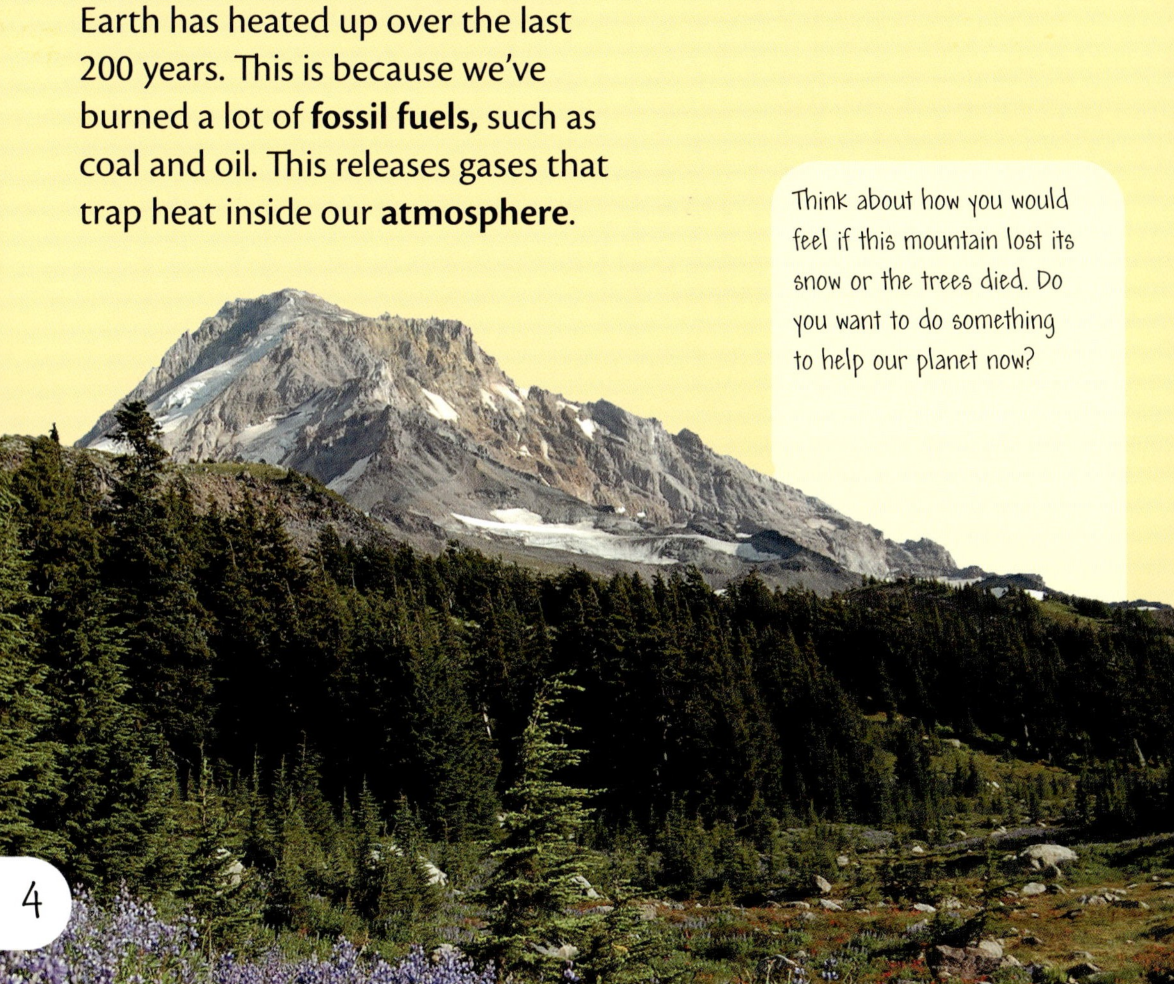

A power plant billows harmful fumes.

What does it mean?

On average, the world's oceans have risen by 4 inches (10 cm) in the last 100 years, and they are still rising. Wild birds and butterflies are disappearing because they don't have food at the right time of year.

What can we do?

We can learn more about how the planet works. We can learn about our **carbon footprint**. That's a measure of the amount of energy we use.

The United Nations Environment Programme (UNEP) can help keep us informed.

What do you know about our planet?

WATER WORRIES

We need to be concerned about water. In some parts of the world there isn't enough water. In other parts, there is just too much.

Wild weather

Weather patterns are changing. In some places, dry periods are lasting much longer. This causes drought. In other places, rainfall has become much heavier. That leads to flooding. Droughts and floods have forced 25 million people across Africa and Asia to move.

What a waste

Broken water pipes can leak huge amounts of water. A dripping faucet can waste 20 gallons (90 liters) of water every week. Water is a precious resource, so why are we wasting it?

Water holes can dry up during a drought, like this one did. With no water to drink, whole herds of **livestock** may die.

Action around the world

It's difficult for many people in **developing countries** to find safe drinking water. CARE and Ryan's Well are two organizations that help people with water needs. You can find out more on their Web sites:
www.care.org/careswork/whatwedo/health/water.asp
www.ryanswell.ca/

WATCH THAT WATER!

Can you guess how much water you use at home? One day, make a note each time you have a drink, turn on a faucet, and flush the toilet. Think about ways of reducing and **recycling** the water you use. Here are some ideas to get you started:

* Turn the faucet off while you are brushing your teeth.
* Wash the car with leftover water from a bath
* Take a short shower instead of a bath.

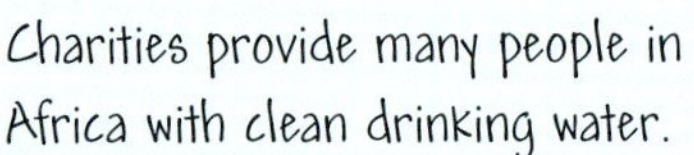

Charities provide many people in Africa with clean drinking water.

FRAGILE FORESTS

Forests and woodlands are being destroyed all over the world. Trees are cut down for firewood and **lumber**. They are also cut down just to clear land for farming.

WHY SHOULD WE SAVE TREES?

* Forests are the lungs of the world. They produce **oxygen** that we breathe.
* The world's forests provide homes for at least 60 percent of all animal and plant **species**.
* They are **habitats** for **bacteria**, **fungi**, and **mosses**, which are important to the process of breaking down plant matter.
* Many forest plants give us important medicines.
* Tree and plant roots hold the soil together and prevent mudslides when it rains.
* Leaves absorb carbon gases that heat up Earth. Less carbon gas in the air helps stop extreme weather.

Action around the world

Many people in developing countries cook on stoves run by clean energy such as **charcoal** or solar power. Many countries are also protecting their forests, as well as planting trees to make new forests.

Solar panels are used to heat water in the home.

What can we do?

On a large piece of recycled paper, make a list of the reasons why trees are so important (like the one on page 8). Hang it up at home or at school to show people why we need to save trees.

Wood is used for making furniture and paper.

FARMING FOREVER

Some types of farming are damaging the planet. We need to think about how we are going to carry on producing food in the future.

What's the problem?

Many **cosmetics**, soaps, and toothpastes are made from palm oil. So, some farmers clear forests to grow palm trees. Other farmers burn grasslands to grow **cereals** to make **biofuels**. Although biofuels burn cleaner than gas and oil, clearing wild areas is damaging to the planet.

These crops are being harvested. They will be used to make biofuel.

Action around the world

We need to buy more food that is grown locally. This food is fresher and less fuel is used to transport it to the store. The Slow Food Movement is an organization that supports locally grown food. It's members educate people about food and how it is grown.

What can we do?

Why not grow your own vegetables in the garden? By growing your own food and buying less from supermarkets, you will help cut down on the distance food must be transported.

Farming begins at home.

Large areas of forest are cut down to grow crops to be made into biofuels.

BETTER BUILDING

Better building makes for a better planet! Building homes and offices in wild places destroys natural habitats.

What's the problem?

- Making building materials, such as **concrete**, use up a lot of energy and water.
- Some builders use **hardwoods** from trees in tropical rain forests. It takes a long time for new trees to grow to replace the ones cut down.
- People build homes on flat plains where rivers flood, which means the homes can also be flooded.

This farmhouse is surrounded by floodwater.

What's the solution?

We can build new houses using **renewable** materials, such as straw bales for insulation. We can also try to fill up all the empty houses before we build new ones.

What's going on near you?

Are there empty houses in your neighborhood? How could the area be planned or built? Write your thoughts in a letter and send it to your local newspaper.

ACTION AROUND THE WORLD

Nader Khalil is an architect who designs houses that are ecofriendly. He uses local materials such as clay and animal dung. These materials are perfect for his dome-shaped houses. These houses are built very quickly, too. This is why they have been used for homeless refugees. There are at least 500 million people without a home in the world today.

Houses in the BedZED project in England use zero energy or energy only from on-site renewable resources.

Solar panels on roofs reduce the need for electricity.

Thick wall insulation keeps in heat and coolness.

Local building materials are used to reduce pollution from transportation. Rainwater is collected, reused, and recycled.

FIGHTING THE FUMES

Take the bus, ride your bike, or walk to school and help stop global warming and climate change.

QUESTION BUSTING!

Q: Aren't we all making too big of a fuss about burning fossil fuels?

A: Absolutely not! Every year, about 7 billion tons (6.5 billion metric tons) of carbon dioxide is put into the air by burning fossil fuels.

Q: Diesel fuel is better than gas, isn't it?

A: Diesel engines burn about 30 percent less fuel than gas engines. So they make 30 percent less carbon dioxide. But diesel engines release soot, which also holds a lot of heat.

Q; Are biofuels better than fossil fuels?

A: Clearning land to grow cereals for biofuels is destroying the environment. Reusing cooking oil for biofuel is a better way to help the environment.

Action around the world

Cooking uses up a lot of fuel. In India, many people cook with biogas made from animal dung or food waste. The gases produced by burning biogas do not harm the planet. In richer parts of the world, cooking in a microwave can save about 70 percent of energy

What can we do?

Carpooling to school can help save the planet because it saves fuel. It also saves time because there is less traffic on the road.

Cycling is good exercise and helps save the planet.

Sharing a car ride can help save the planet.

THINK ABOUT TOURISM

Hurray— it's vacation time! But the planet isn't cheering. Long trips to faraway places add to our carbon footprints. Many tourist resorts are spoiling natural environments. It's time to rethink how we spend our leisure time.

THINK IT THROUGH!

One trip on an airplane can't hurt, can it? Well, it depends how far you go. If you fly from New York to London, you help to pump out about 1.5 tons (1.4 metric tons) of carbon dioxide, as well as other harmful gases.

Airlines are using more planes and bigger planes to cope with all the passengers. New runways and air terminals are spreading across the world. Building them uses precious energy.

Air travel is adding to the pollution problem.

Action around the world

Tourism is good because it gives people jobs. But there is a flip side. Tourists use up local water and energy and create a lot of waste.

You can still go on vacation and help the planet. Some people go on vacation to clean up the countryside, trim hedges, fix fences, and clear ditches. This is called ecotourism, and it can be a lot of fun.

Beautiful coral reefs like this one are damaged by sewage from hotels.

What can we do?

Make the most of where you live. Visit new places that are within walking distance or a bicycle ride away. Find out about the history of your local area. Write down what you find out and draw some of the things you see. You could make a brochure for your local tourist information center or library.

Find out your local history.

Make the most of where you live.

DRASTIC PLASTC

Plastic can be very useful, but it is polluting our planet. From bags and bottles to packaging and radios, plastic trash is everywhere.

Plastic hazards

Plastic can be bad news. It is made from petroleum, and smelly fumes fill the air when plastic is made. These fumes are bad for our health and can damage the atmosphere.

Plastic bottles take thousands of years to break down in landfill sites. Plastic bags choke birds, mammals, and sea creatures. They can also block drains and cause floods.

Waste around the world

Every year, people throw away four billion plastic bags. Tied end to end, this many bags would circle Earth an amazing 63 times!

Many birds die each year because they eat plastic trash.

SAVE THE PLANET

Plastic trash is everywhere, so pick it up and try to reuse it.

* Show people just how many plastic bottles are thrown away each week by making a sculpture out of your household's bottles.
* Use a reusable water bottle for your drinking water.
* REUSE plastic bags or just REFUSE them.
* Bangladesh has banned plastic bags. We could do it, too!

Slick slogans

Slogans sell ideas. Think of some short, snappy slogans to point out the problems of plastic. You could try the slogans below.

"I am the problem. I am the solution."

Reduce, reuse, recycle!

SMALL STEPS, GIANT LEAPS

There are a lot of things you can do to save the environment. You have read about some of them in this book. Every little change makes a big difference to our planet.

What's the problem?

The world is warming up. Winters are milder, and spring flowers bloom earlier. The warm ground whips up stronger tornadoes, and warm oceans contribute to devastating hurricanes. These things are happening in front of our eyes, so no one can deny that there is a problem. The next step is to do something about it.

Plant a tree! Trees will absorb harmful carbon gases.

What's the solution?

Let's reduce the amount of waste we produce. Reduce what we use, reuse what we have, and remember to recycle. We can do all these at home, at school, and on vacation. These small steps will help save energy and save the planet. It really is that easy.

LET'S BEGIN AT HOME!

Now that you have read this book, think about all the things you can do to make a difference. Write a list. Here's a start:

* Take a short shower instead of a bath.
* Turn the faucet off while you are brushing your teeth.
* Use energy-saving lightbulbs, such as the one shown at right.
* Walk or cycle if you can.
* Reduce, reuse, recycle.
* Grow some herbs or vegetables.

You'll feel much better for it.
You are helping to save our planet!

GLOSSARY

atmosphere The upper layer of gases around Earth

bacteria Tiny living cells. Some cause disease. Others clear up harmful waste

biofuels Fuels made from crops such as corn and palm oil

carbon dioxide A "greenhouse gas" released by burning fossil fuels. It forms a layer of gases around Earth that trap heat inside our atmosphere

carbon footprint The amount of energy each person uses

cereals Foods from the seeds of grasses, such as corn, millet, and wheat

charcoal Slowly burned, charred wood. Charcoal is used for fuel and lasts longer than wood

concrete A hard building material made by mixing cement, sand, gravel, and water

cosmetics Creams, lotions, and makeup used by people

developing countries Nations with economies that do not provide good standards of living to its citizens

fossil fuels Fuels, such as coal and oil, made from the remains of ancient life-forms

fungi A puffy growth a bit like a plant. Mushrooms are fungi

habitats Types of natural area, such as rain forests or grasslands

hardwoods Slow-growing trees that take a long time to replace

livestock Animals reared for food, such as cattle and sheep

mosses Masses of tiny, plantlike leaves that make a soft, velvety covering

oxygen A gas that humans and creatures take in and use to keep their bodies working

recycling Using something in a different way

renewable Something that can be used over and over again

species Type of plant or creature

lumber Wood prepared for use in construction as well as making furniture, paper, and other products

FURTHER INFORMATION

Web sites

This fun site from the U.S. Environmental Protection Agency has games and animation to teach children about climate change:
http://epa.gov/climatechange/kids/

This Web site provides great links for kids on global warming, climate change, and what we can do to help:
http://globalwarmingkids.net/

Take environmental activist David Suzuki's Nature Challenge for Kids—10 fun and easy things we can do together to protect nature!
www.davidsuzuki.org/kids/

Find tips on "go green", recycling, ecotourism, and food at:
www.ecofriendlykids.co.uk

This gives lots of rain forest facts, games, and news:
www.kidssavingtherainforest.org/factsheet.php.htm

Find loads of facts on energy sources and how they affect the environment at:
http://tonto.eia.doe.gov/kids/

Books

Energy Revolution Series. Crabtree Publishing Company (2010)
Environment Action Series. Crabtree Publishing Company (2008)
Green Team Series. Crabtree Publishing Company (2009)
Protecting our Planet Series. Crabtree Publishing Company (2010)

INDEX